Gus' Fortunate Misfortune

By Susan Pepka

Illustrated By Joseph Cowman

"I'm TRAPPED!" Gus cried to himself.

Stuck inside a closed box, Gus felt more afraid than ever before.

"This is awful," he thought.

"How will I ever get out of this mess?"

Looking for a way out, Gus searched every inch of the box.

He found odd bits of old and broken teacups and mugs . . . But no way out.

Arrgh . . . .
If only that muffin hadn't smelled so good!
He'd just wanted a nibble.
And if only that cat hadn't shown up right as he was taking a bite.

It all happened so fast, the wooden box had seemed like the best place to hide.
And then, if only that human hadn't closed the box trapping him inside.

"Now here I am." he thought.

"Alone in the dark. I'm hungry. I'm scared.
Any minute now I'm going to die!"

Terrified, Gus huddled in a corner of the box trembling from the
point of his little pink nose to the tip of his quivering tail.

Feeling fear was not a new emotion for Gus.
It seemed like he'd grown up feeling afraid.

Being smaller and slower than most other mice his age, bigger mice often used Gus as a target.
They made fun of him, poking him with their noses and biting his tail.
Gus spent a lot of his time alone, hiding from those bullies.

Then there were the cats. Always prowling, looking for a mouse that wasn't being mindful. Gus heard horrible stories of what might happen to a naughty mouse caught by a cat. He shuddered to think of it.

His parents had taught him to be wary of humans who would set traps intended just for mice!! His mother warned him to never go near one of those traps, no matter how hungry he was. He might not get out of it.

Lonely, afraid, and finally exhausted Gus fell asleep.

He dreamed that he was home, safe with his family.
He was wrestling with his brother and sister.
His parents watched over them lovingly.
Everyone was laughing. It was a really good time.

If only this dream were real.

The box tilted
roughly and Gus woke
abruptly from his dream.
He heard sounds and voices.

A car door closed.
Gus had definitely been taken
somewhere. He heard people laughing,
and finally the box was set down.

Hearing laughter reminded Gus of his family.
How he wished to be home again!

Small tears fell from his eyes and he wiped
them away with his little paw.

So sad. So scared.

What would happen now?

Gus felt the box move and then the top opened flooding the insides with bright light.
Gus managed to lift and scurry under a teacup just in time!

A hand reached into the box, took something out, and then all was quiet.
His heart was pounding so hard from fright, he thought he'd die right then and there!

Then he remembered that the box was open.
Courageously he lifted the teacup and peaked out.

He waited.
He listened.
He sniffed.

He didn't THINK any
danger was lurking.

Best of all, he wasn't
trapped anymore!

"I'M SAVED!!" he thought.

But where was he?

Poking his head just barely out of the box, Gus took his first look around.

Everything was strange.

He didn't know where he was but at least he couldn't see or smell any cats or humans.

With knees quaking and whiskers quivering Gus decided it was time to explore.

Gripping the box edge with his teeth and pulling and pushing with all four paws Gus grappled his way out of the box.

Peeking around a corner of the box he saw that he was in a room that seemed familiar.

He saw a table, some cupboards, and a small refrigerator.

And the way was clear.

So far, so good.
He relaxed a little.

Then his tummy rumbled loudly and Gus remembered how hungry he was!
His nose twitched.

Time to look for food.

Now the best way for a mouse to find food is to follow its nose.

Gus sniffed to the left. He sniffed to the right.

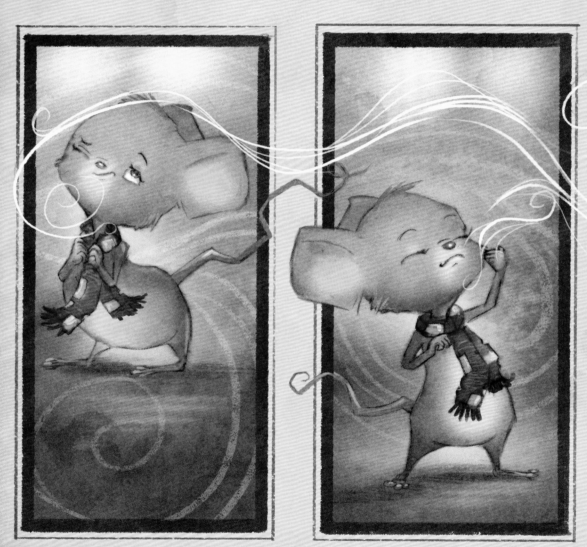
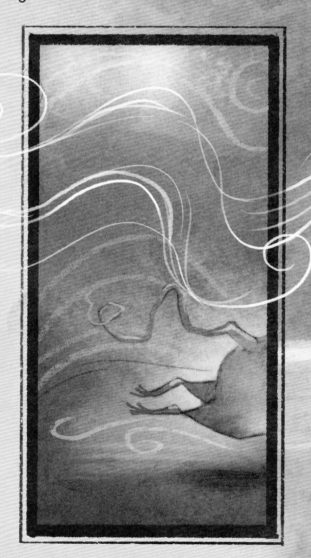

Then he caught a scent of something . . . different . . . unfamiliar.

Scurrying along the edge of the wall he
searched for the source of that smell.

Scritch, Scratch.

His claws made a small noise as
he crept along. Following that odd
scent he came to a door.

Sniff.

The smell was definitely
coming from behind the door.

How to get in?

Gus scratched with his paw.

Quicker than a blink the door opened
and a large foot appeared!

18

Gus barely had enough time to turn
tail and scamper back the way he'd come.
Desperately he looked for a safe hiding place.
All he found was a tiny crack between a
cupboard and the refrigerator.

Gus dove for cover.

He squeezed as hard as he could to not be seen
. . . pushing and pushing . . .
but the space was just too small. Gus could only squeeze
in his head and shoulders.
Quivering and quaking
he prayed that enough of him was hidden.

Gus did not know that the place he found himself was the
kitchen of a Buddhist temple and the person who had
opened the door was a monk named Jamyang.

Jamyang's name meant "gentle voice" and he was known for his kindness.
When he spotted Gus trying to hide he realized that the mouse must be terrified.
He thought of what he might do to help Gus not feel so fearful.

He saw an opened bag of chips and thought he could offer
Gus a snack. He crumbled some up and set them on the floor.
Slowly backing far away, he waited where he could
see what Gus would do.

A minute passed.

Then another.

Two more minutes crept by before Gus felt safe
enough to leave that small space.

Besides, he'd heard the sound of chips
crunching and remembered his tummy!

Jamyang found the
waiting difficult.
He wondered,
"Why doesn't the
mouse hurry up!"

Then remembering what
he'd been taught about being
patient, Jamyang took
some deep breaths and
stilled himself.

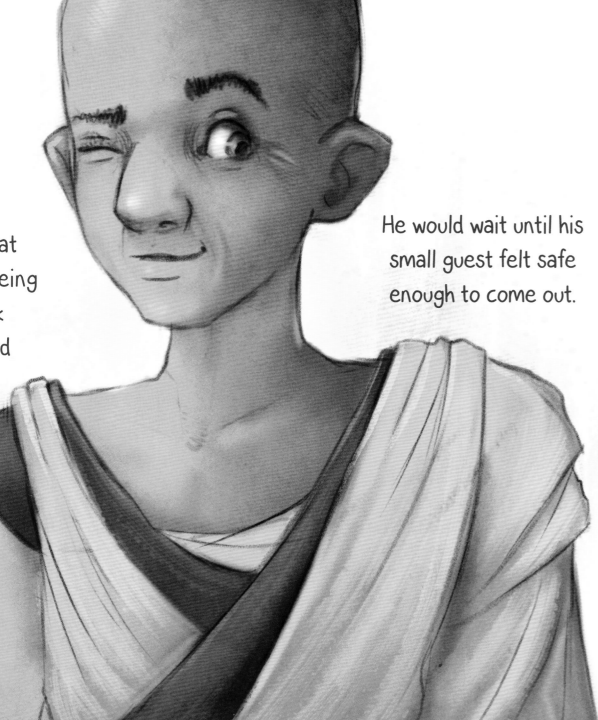

He would wait until his
small guest felt safe
enough to come out.

Wiggling his backside and swishing his tail, Gus made sure there wasn't anything behind him.

He slowly backed out of his hiding place, being careful not to make any sound.

Sniff, sniff, sniff.
Gus located the chips and hungrily scrambled over to them!.

Munch . . . crunch.

Oh, they were so good!

It was like heaven to have food in his tummy again!
He munched and crunched some more.

Tummy full, Gus felt thirsty enough to drink a river.
His next mission was to find water.

After watching Gus gobble up the chips, Jamyang went back to his small room to begin studying and meditating.

Jamyang had a small shrine there with statues of Buddha and other precious objects.

Some incense burned, wafting a soothing scent into the room. There were also seven small bowls filled with water which represent offerings to holy beings.

Jamyang settled himself on his meditation cushion.
Closing his eyes, he began to relax and quiet his thoughts.

He often found this difficult because he was so easily distracted. He sometimes found himself thinking of what he wanted to eat for dinner.

Or sometimes he'd think about what a fine day it was for a long walk in the forest.

Today thoughts of a very small visitor to the temple were distracting him.

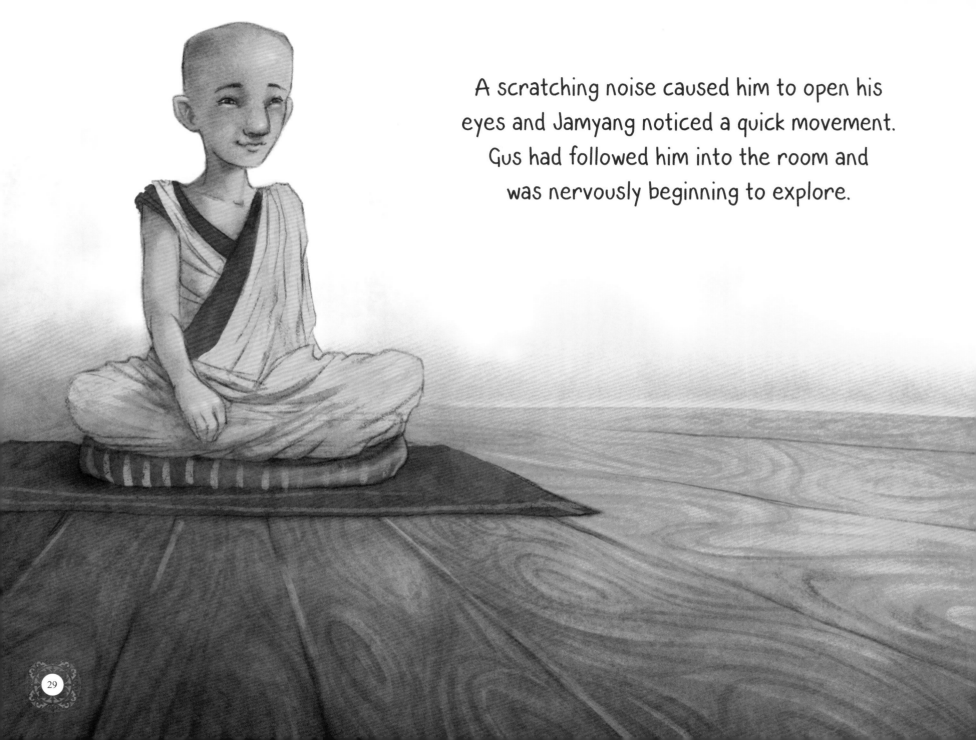

A scratching noise caused him to open his eyes and Jamyang noticed a quick movement. Gus had followed him into the room and was nervously beginning to explore.

Curious to see what Gus would do,
and not wanting to frighten him,
Jamyang stayed very still on his cushion.

He once again needed to practice being
patient as the small mouse zigzagged
around the few bits of furniture
in the room.

In his quest for water, Gus made his way back to the monk's room.
The door was ajar and Gus squeezed into the room.

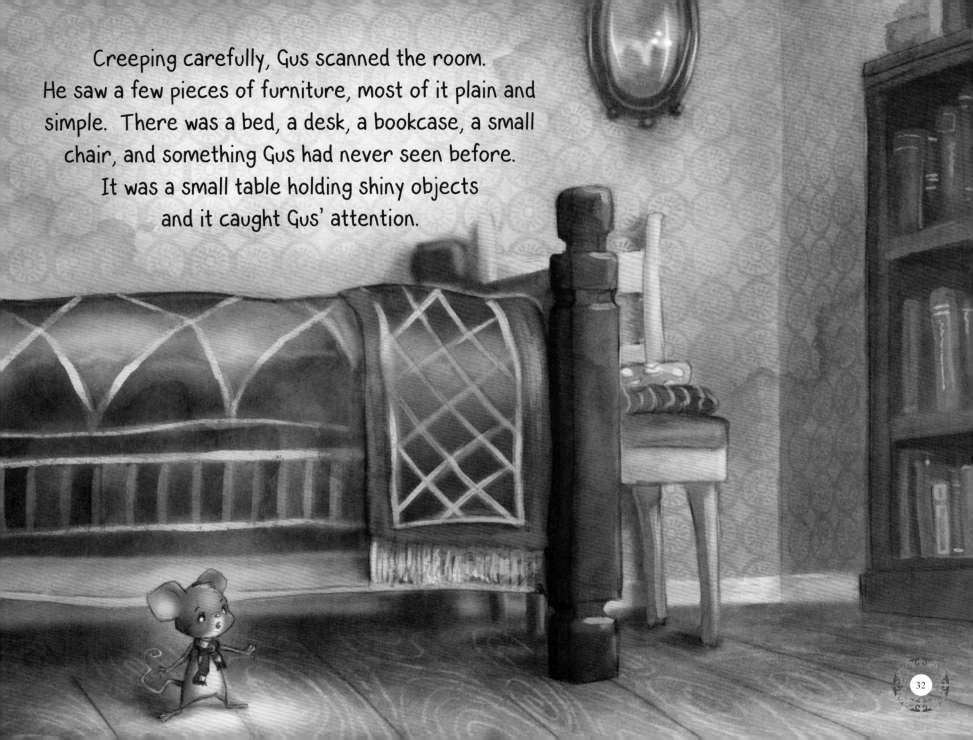

Creeping carefully, Gus scanned the room.
He saw a few pieces of furniture, most of it plain and
simple. There was a bed, a desk, a bookcase, a small
chair, and something Gus had never seen before.
It was a small table holding shiny objects
and it caught Gus' attention.

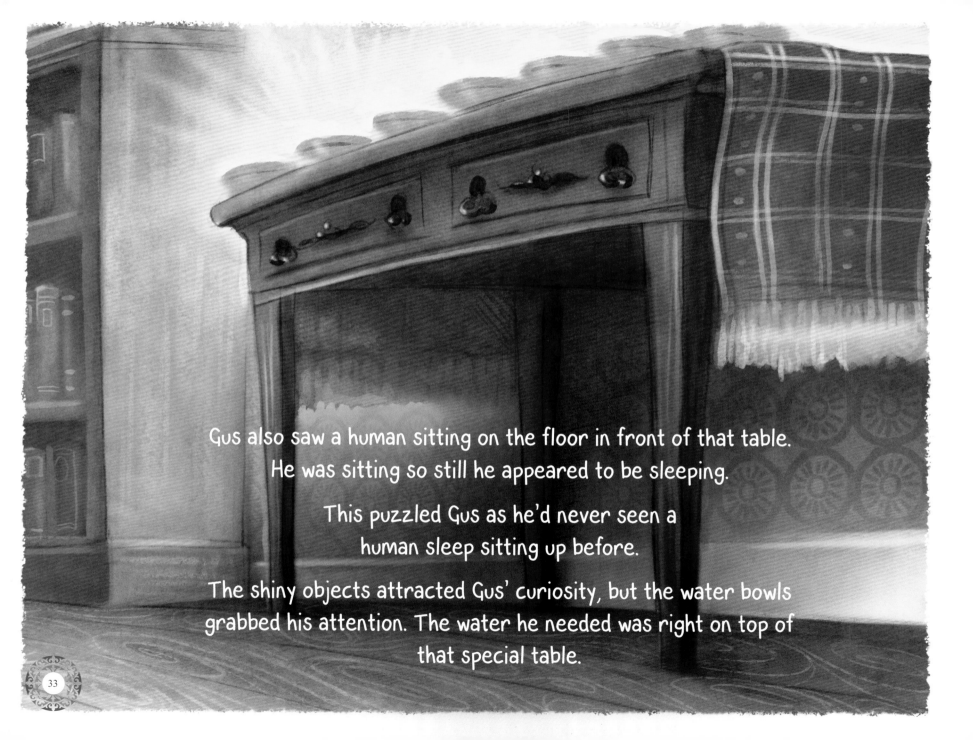

Gus also saw a human sitting on the floor in front of that table.
He was sitting so still he appeared to be sleeping.

This puzzled Gus as he'd never seen a
human sleep sitting up before.

The shiny objects attracted Gus' curiosity, but the water bowls
grabbed his attention. The water he needed was right on top of
that special table.

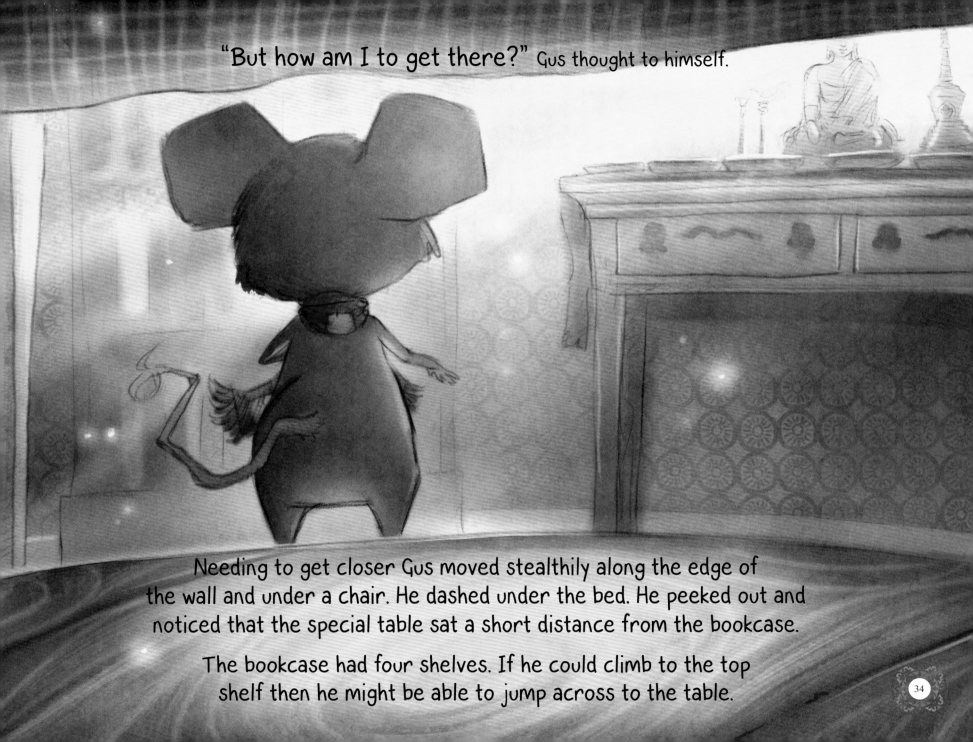

"But how am I to get there?" Gus thought to himself.

Needing to get closer Gus moved stealthily along the edge of the wall and under a chair. He dashed under the bed. He peeked out and noticed that the special table sat a short distance from the bookcase.

The bookcase had four shelves. If he could climb to the top shelf then he might be able to jump across to the table.

This was bigger than anything Gus had ever done before.
He didn't know exactly how he was going to accomplish it,
he just knew he had to.

Taking a big, deep breath Gus decided
there was no time like now.

Scurrying to the bookcase,
he reached the bottom shelf
searching for a way up.
Finding nothing to grab on to,
Gus started to stretch and stretch,
making himself as tall as possible.
Reaching as far as he could he
finally had a grip on the shelf.

Now to pull himself up.

Getting a little bounce in
his feet and legs, then
concentrating with all his
might Gus pushed off.
He managed to barely
catapult himself up onto
the second shelf.

36

Catching his breath, Gus glanced over at the young monk.
He appeared to be still sleeping although Gus thought he saw a bit of
twitching around his mouth. Seeing no other movement Gus continued on.

Getting to the next two shelves was going to be more difficult, but Gus had to concentrate on just one of them for now. No matter how Gus stretched he couldn't reach the shelf above. He would have to find another way.

He ran to one end of the shelf looking for a way up. He found none.

He tried the other end.

Nothing there either.

What was he to do?

Then Gus noticed space between the books on the shelf and the underside of the shelf above. Grabbing hold of a book he pulled himself up.

Then, laying on his back, he reached way out and up to grab hold of the upper edge. Reaching and stretching as far as he could he gripped the shelf with one paw.

Taking a deep breath he flung himself off the book and into the air.

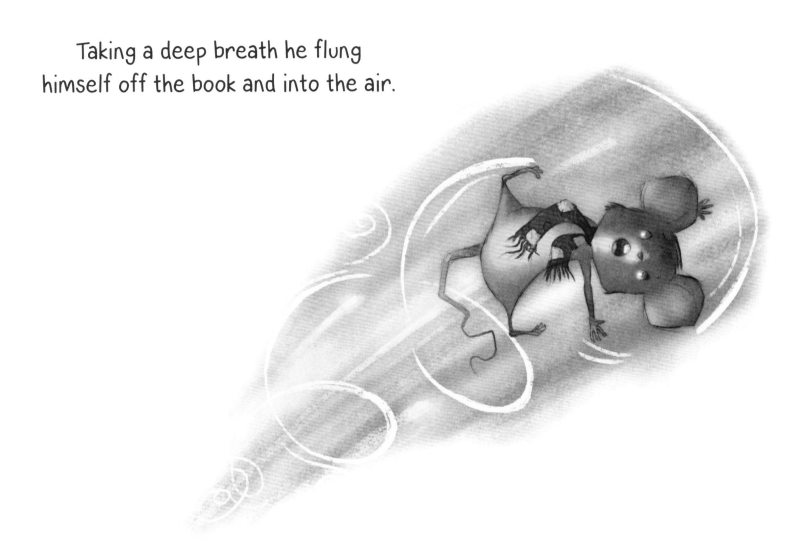

But his hold wasn't strong enough and, with a loud clunk,
Gus fell back down to the lower shelf.

Oof!

His breath knocked out of him, Gus lay there hoping once more that the monk still slept.

He glanced over.
No movement except that for a second he
thought he had seen the monk's eyes
get very big and round.

Time to try again. Gus easily jumped onto another book.

Again he reached out with his right paw. Stretch . . . stretch . . . grab hold . . .
dig his claws in . . . really get a good hold.

Now, with all his strength Gus pushed himself off of the books.
This time he managed to get his left paw onto the edge.
Only now he was hanging in midair! How to get his bottom up?

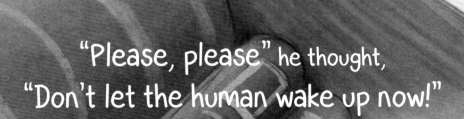

"Please, please" he thought,
"Don't let the human wake up now!"

Gus' little arms were tiring fast and
he knew he had to do something before he fell.

He wiggled his legs and swung from side to side.
Each swing brought him a bit closer to the top.

Then one final swing and giving it all he had he
flung himself onto the shelf above.

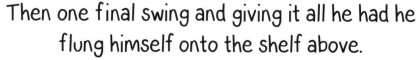

Whew, he made it!!

Now only one more shelf to climb. Gus was so tired he wasn't sure he had
enough strength left. "Please, please help me," he thought.
"I don't think I can do this on my own."

An image of Gus' mom came to his mind.
She had always told him that he could do
anything if he set his heart and mind to it.
It was time to see if she was right!

Pulling himself together he climbed on top of the books.

Looking around Gus was hoping to find something to help him finish his climb. There in the corner he saw a lumpy knot of wood that looked big enough to use as a foot hold. Stretching, he planted his foot on the wood then reached with his paw to grasp the shelf above. Trying to not think of how weak he felt or how high up he was Gus pushed with his foot and pulled with his paws and dragged himself onto the top of the bookcase.

Resting a moment to regain some strength, Gus had no energy to see what the monk was doing.

All he knew was that he now had to jump across to the special table.

Gus moved cautiously to the edge. He sighted the distance.

Was it too far for him to jump?

What if he missed?

There was no other way though.

He'd have to make it!

He needed a running start. Scampering all the way to the opposite end he took a deep breath. Steadying himself, he began running. As the edge grew closer he felt a little sick in his stomach.

Closer now . . . almost there . . . no turning back now!

Gus was inches from the edge and picking up speed.
"You can do this!" he thought.

Almost . . . almost . . . NOW!

Reaching the edge he pushed
off with all his might.

He was flying!

He could see the special
table and prayed that
he'd make it.

Got it!

With claws catching hold of the tablecloth, he
held on for all he was worth.
One more push and pull and Gus
had reached his goal!

Needing water badly now Gus quickly
found it in several small bowls sitting
in front of a shiny statue.
He tasted from the first bowl.

Ah, so refreshing!

Then the next and the next until
he'd dipped his nose into each of
the seven bowls.

Finally, he was satisfied.

Gus paused to look around now and see what was on this special table.
In addition to the bowls of water there was a large, shiny statue of a person.
Gus knew he'd never seen this person before and yet he felt so
calm just looking into his face.

There were other items also.
A book and some flowers.
A shiny crystal and a statue
that looked like a tower.

55

Gus was curious and wanted to explore but then he remembered that he wasn't alone in the room. Was the human still sleeping?

Gus looked and saw that the monk's eyes were wide open and he was looking straight back at Gus with a puzzled look on his face.

56

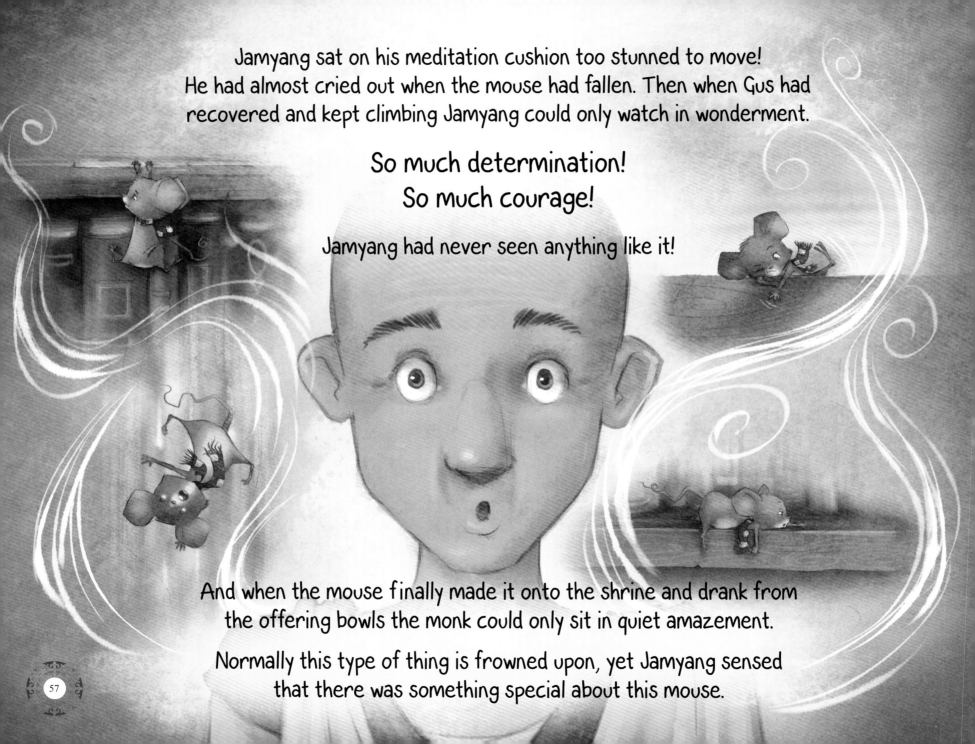

Jamyang sat on his meditation cushion too stunned to move!
He had almost cried out when the mouse had fallen. Then when Gus had recovered and kept climbing Jamyang could only watch in wonderment.

So much determination!
So much courage!

Jamyang had never seen anything like it!

And when the mouse finally made it onto the shrine and drank from the offering bowls the monk could only sit in quiet amazement.

Normally this type of thing is frowned upon, yet Jamyang sensed that there was something special about this mouse.

Taking no more chances, Gus decided it was time to exit.
Finding an easy way down and spotting a crack in the wall,
Gus discovered a small place where he could sleep.

That evening, after all the lights were out and the temple was quiet,
Gus ventured out of his hiding place. There, waiting for him, was a slice of cheese,
a few bits of cracker, and a small dish of water. Nearby was a bit of flannel just the right
size for a warm and snuggly blanket. He was reminded about his family, and how he wished they
were with him, but he was now confident that he could manage on his own.
He even thought he'd make some new friends.

After nibbling on the cheese and crackers, and taking a few sips of water, Gus happily pulled the blanket into his little corner. With a satisfied sigh Gus realized he had found his new home.

And he was safe.

Written by Susan Pepka

A native of Detroit and currently living in Atlanta, Susan Pepka has enjoyed great diversity throughout her life. Mother of three and grandmother of four, Susan has experienced life as a preschool teacher, technologist in diagnostic imaging, co-owner of a successful wellness center, meditation teacher, and now a published author with the debut of her first children's book, Gus' Fortunate Misfortune.

One of Susan's greatest pleasures is reading wonderful stories that stir the imagination and nourish the spirit. Her passion is helping others find ways to healthier, happier, and more meaningful lives. Her wish is that all beings live together in harmony.

Illustrated by Joseph Cowman

Joseph shares his Boise Idaho home with his wife, who is an amazing high school teacher and writer of children's stories, a daughter Savannah who finds the world fascinating and beautiful at every turn, a daughter Alina who can be found building a garden all through the year, a son Phoenix who makes magic because he believes in it, Olive; a lazy gentle Basset hound, and Gibbs the fish who was recently renamed Nubs because he lost a fin.

Gus' Fortunate Misfortune

Cover, interior illustrations by Joseph Cowman • Cover and interior design by Ted Ruybal

ISBN: 978-0-9966422-3-1
LCCN: 2018932024
Registration Number: TXu 1-942-741

JUV002180   JUVENILE FICTION / Animals / Mice, Hamsters, Guinea Pigs, etc.

Printed in China / 100% recycled paper

Quality reading and entertainment

www.fullcyclepublications.com
P. O. Box 57005, Murray, Utah 84157
Tel: 1 (801) 299-2705 • Fax: 1 (801) 905-3348 • Email: info@fullcyclepublications.com